D1270729

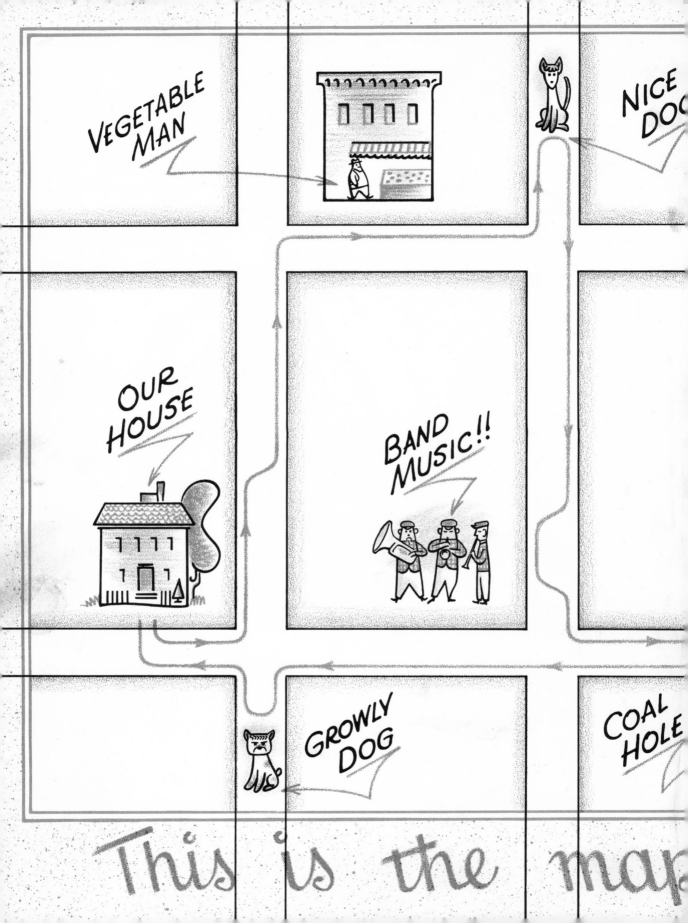

VEGETABLE MAN

NICE DOG

OUR HOUSE

BAND MUSIC!!

GROWLY DOG

COAL HOLE

This is the map

A Walk in the City

A WALK
in the
CITY

by Rosemary and Richard Dawson

THE VIKING PRESS · NEW YORK

Southmoreland Elementary Library

All rights reserved

Copyright 1950 by Rosemary and Richard Dawson

Published by the Viking Press in April 1950

Published on the same day in the Dominion of Canada

by The Macmillan Company of Canada Limited

Tenth printing June 1970

Pic Bk

VLB 670–74910–9

Lithographed in the United States of America

By Reehl Litho Company

For Marjory and Bill

We live in a house in the city

As happy as we can be,

With things around us to listen to

And things in the streets to see.

And while Daddy's at work we go walking,

My Mommy, my wagon, and me.

The houses stand up all around us

On streets that are long and wide,

And sometimes through the windows

We can see the people inside.

So we talk about what they're doing

While I'm giving my wagon a ride.

There are lots of dogs in the city,

Seven or nine or ten,

And the nice ones wag their tails and jump

And are happy to see us when

We come along — but the bad ones bark,

And we won't speak to them again.

The man who lives at the corner

Has a friendly grocery store,

And we look at the apples and carrots and grapes

When we're going by his door.

And sometimes he gives me an apple,

Because that's what he has them for.

Or we see some men who are tooting

On horns as shiny as toys,

Making lots of thumping music

For grown-ups and girls and boys.

And all the way to the end of the street

We can hear their big loud noise.

We walk by the dark little window

That looks down into a hole,

There's a man inside with a shovel

Who digs in the dark like a mole.

And that's the place where the big black truck

Is pouring in lots of coal.

Sometimes, when it's warm in the city,

There's a better surprise than the band —

The organ man comes down the street

And his music is almost as grand.

I can give the monkey a penny,

And he'll put his paw in my hand!

Southmoreland Elementary Library

We see the big green busses

With the people going away,

And then we wave good-by to them,

And maybe the driver will say

That he wishes we were coming, too,

But we tell him we can't today.

The iceman is very busy

With a wagon that's clean and new,

But he always stops for a minute

So he can talk to you.

And he puts some ice in my wagon,

And then I'm an iceman, too.

The nicest thing in the city

Is the park where I go every day,

With a fence going round outside it

And a place inside to stay.

I can climb on everything I like,

And play what I want to play.

We all bring things to play with,

So I bring my wagon that's red,

And have fun with the other children

Till it's time for supper and bed.

And Mommy tells me we're going home

And calls me a sleepy-head.

And then we walk home in the city

As tired as we can be,

And talk about what to tell Daddy

About all the people we see,

About all the streets and the houses

That my Mommy shows to me.

There is our house on the corner,

With our door and our little green tree,

And we finish telling each other things

And open the door with the key.

We're all tired out at the end of the day,

My Mommy, my wagon, and me.

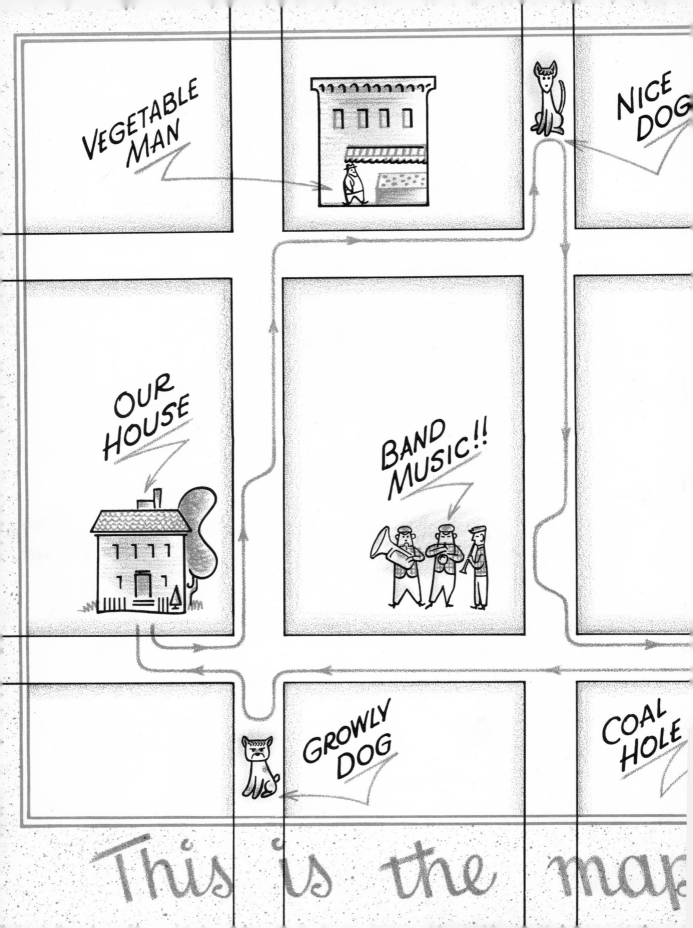

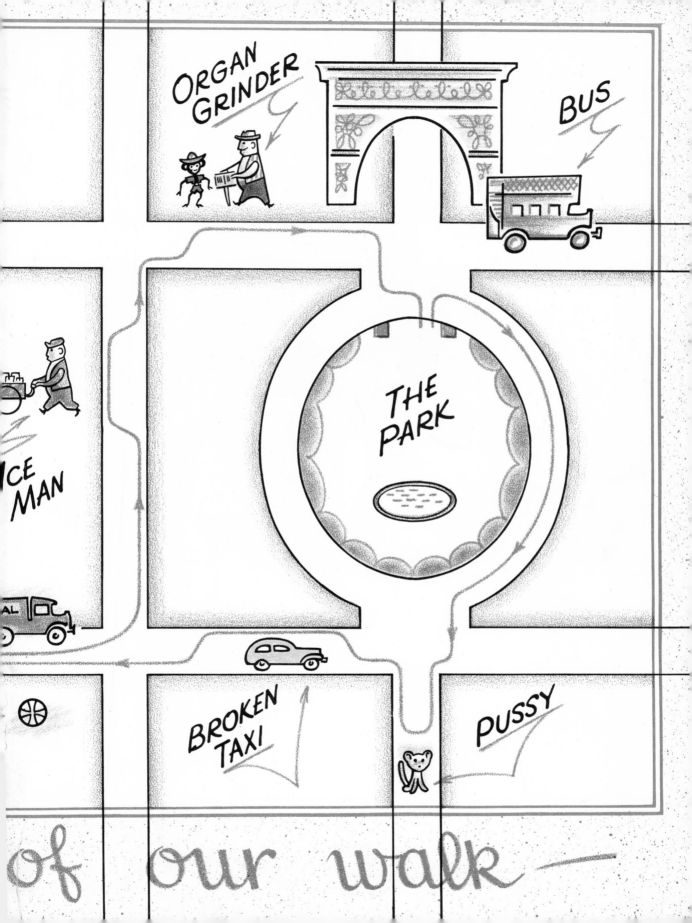